Buttercup

Butterfly

Chickadee

Columbine

Cornflower

Forget-me-not

Golden rod

Jewelweed

Joe-pye-weed

Johnny-jump-up

Marigold

Milkweed

Mockingbird

Morning Glory

Mum

Praying Mantis

Queen Anne's Lace

Robin

Rose

Slug

Sweet William

Thistle

Violet

Worm

Zinnia

For Rose and Jenna,
my consultants

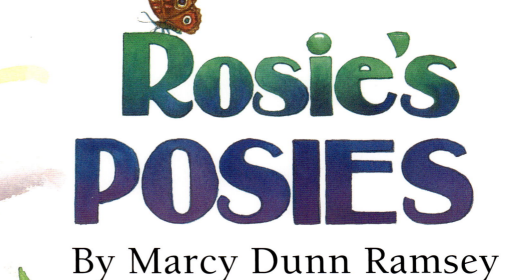

Rosie's POSIES

By Marcy Dunn Ramsey

Tidewater Publishers
Centreville, Maryland 21617

Rosie watched the rain turn to snow. Outside it was cold, and she felt lonely in this new place. Her dad was taking care of a big farm on the Eastern Shore of Maryland, and there were no other children close by.

She sighed and went to sit by the fire with her mother.

"What's that?" she asked.

"It's a seed catalog. I'm planning what to grow in our garden this spring. Would you like to help?"

"Oh, yes!" she nodded. Her eyes lit up when she looked at all the bright pages.

"Corn and tomatoes, beans and potatoes, spinach and squash and honeydew, zukes and cukes, lettuce and leeks, peppers and peas and cantaloupe, too," read her mom.

HAPPY HARVEST!

Then Rosie saw the flower section and squeaked, "I see my name!"

"Yes," said her mom, "there are lots of beautiful roses! And see what else we could grow — asters, daisies, pansies and black-eyed Susans, columbines, zinnias, sunflowers and snapdragons, sweet peas, sweet William, petunias and poppies, marigolds and mums, bachelor's buttons, Johnny-jump-ups and nasturtiums."

FLOWERS

ROSES

see page 42

Rosie waited patiently for the seeds to come in the mail . . .

Finally, the mail lady left a fat package in their box, just as the days were getting longer and the ground was beginning to thaw.

Rosie and her mom put on their work clothes and boots one mild spring day and set out to start their garden.

First they turned over the earth with their shovels and then they mixed in bits of dead leaves, grass, and kitchen scraps from the compost pile to enrich the soil. "It looks like chocolate cake," said Rosie.

"Well, don't eat it! It's food for the *plants*, not for you!" said her mom.

Then they marked out rows and began to plant the tiny seeds.

Rain and sun and seven days passed quickly by. One damp morning Rosie ran out to see if anything had sprouted.

Sure enough, little green seedlings were poking up their heads.

Soon the warm sun coaxed *everybody* up!

Rosie's mom was busy tending the vegetables.
Rosie pretended the flowers were *her* babies.

As the garden grew, her babies got bigger and more demanding. She weeded and hoed and watered them tenderly.

By July the sunflowers had grown into a great green and golden wall. Birds came to perch on their giant heads.

Rosie's garden was her make-believe world. She was the queen and all the flowers were her loyal subjects.

The wildflowers in the pasture were part of her kingdom, and she learned all their names, too: buttercups, morning glory, milkweed, Joe-pye-weed, thistle, Queen Anne's lace, cornflowers, knotweed, goldenrod, dandelions, daylilies, and forget-me-nots.

In the woods they found lady's slippers, lily-of-the-valley, Solomon's seal, Dutchman's-breeches, violets, and jewelweed.

Sometimes danger threatened her kingdom.
"This witchgrass is *wicked!* Would you help me root
it out, Rosie?"

Rosie felt like SUPERWOMAN!

Then a swarm of bad beetles invaded and had to be bottled.

Slimy slugs had to be tricked into traps.

Soon the birds came to help. Orioles, swallows, robins, bluebirds, chickadees, and even a mockingbird made tasty meals out of the bad bugs.

And there were good critters, too, that helped to keep the garden pest-free: ladybugs, praying mantises, lacewings, worms, and toads. Bees and butterflies came to pollinate the flowers.

By late summer the garden had reached its peak.
It was a blooming bouquet that filled Rosie's fantasies,
and she never felt shy or lonely there.

Then the days began to grow shorter and summer vacation was nearly over.

In September it was time for Rosie's first ride on a schoolbus and her first day of kindergarten.

When she got to her classroom she was feeling shy, but as she looked around at all the new faces something about them seemed familiar.

She really didn't feel shy at all! In fact she felt
right at home!

Gardening Tips

❀ Plant your garden where it will get 6–8 hours of sun a day.

❀ Use a shovel or pitchfork (with a grown-up) to dig up the soil when the warm spring weather has dried the ground out a little. Pull out grass and weed roots.

❀ Plant seeds after the last frost in your area. Where Rosie lives in Maryland, that is usually in April. Follow the directions on the seed packet for depth of planting and spacing of seeds.

❀ Keep your seedbed moist and it will sprout in 7–10 days. After that, water the garden once a week unless there is a good soaking rain.

❀ Thin the seedlings so they don't crowd each other.

❀ Carefully pluck weeds out *by the roots* as they appear.

❀ Put mulch (hay or straw) between the rows to keep the soil moist and weeds out.

❀ If you get bugs in your garden, try not to use pesticides. Just pick off the bugs in a jar or pull the damaged plants.

❀ Pick your flowers often so more buds will form. Use *scissors* to cut them, and make sure you cut lots of stem with your flower.

❀ Give bouquets to your family, friends, and teachers to sweeten their summer days. They will be so proud of you!

Aster	Bachelor's Button	Bee	Black-eyed Susan	Bluebird
Cosmos	Daisy	Dandelion	Daylily	Dutchman's Breeches
Knotweed	Lacewing	Ladybug	Lady's Slipper	Lily of the Valley
Nasturtium	Oriole	Pansy	Petunia	Poppy
Snapdragon	Solomon's Seal	Sunflower	Swallow	Sweet Pea